A native of New York, her career has been in radio and newspaper advertising, mostly sales and copywriting. Her previous novel, *The Spider Who Blew Bubbles*, was for children's enjoyment. Presently, she is hard at work on another novel.

To Mom and Dad. Wish you both
were here to make you proud.

Marianne V. Martino

Trailer Trash

Austin Macauley Publishers
LONDON * CAMBRIDGE * NEW YORK * SHARJAH

Copyright © Marianne V. Martino 2024

All rights reserved. No part of this publication may be reproduced, distributed, or transmitted in any form or by any means, including photocopying, recording, or other electronic or mechanical methods, without the prior written permission of the publisher, except in the case of brief quotations embodied in critical reviews and certain other non-commercial uses permitted by copyright law. For permission requests, write to the publisher.

Any person who commits any unauthorized act in relation to this publication may be liable to criminal prosecution and civil claims for damages.

This is a work of fiction. Names, characters, businesses, places, events, locales, and incidents are either the products of the author's imagination or used in a fictitious manner. Any resemblance to actual persons, living or dead, or actual events is purely coincidental.

Ordering Information
Quantity sales: Special discounts are available on quantity purchases by corporations, associations, and others. For details, contact the publisher at the address below.

Publisher's Cataloging-in-Publication data
Martino, Marianne V.
Trailer Trash

ISBN 9781638290872 (Paperback)
ISBN 9781638290919 (Hardback)
ISBN 9781638290926 (ePub e-book)

Library of Congress Control Number: 2024910668

www.austinmacauley.com/us

First Published 2024
Austin Macauley Publishers LLC
40 Wall Street, 33rd Floor, Suite 3302
New York, NY 10005 USA

mail-usa@austinmacauley.com
+1 (646) 5125767

Chapter 1

I was awakened by the slappin' sound of the screen door closin'. I knew it was momma comin' home from work. The fan blowin' on me at the head of my bed, didn't do nothin' but blow the hot air around and around and flutter the spider webs on the ceilin' like sheets on a clothesline on a hot summer day. As a matter of fact, my sheet was stickin' to me right now, like a piece of gum on the bottom of my flip flops. I could hear momma and Uncle John laughin' and talkin' in the livin' room, and an occasional clink when they whacked their beer bottles together like they were toastin' somethin'.

I got up and went down the narrow, paneled hallway into the livin' room. Momma was sittin' on Uncle John's lap. They were smokin' cigarettes, kissin' and drinkin' beer. They both jumped when they saw me standin' there.

Momma always called me 'honey bunny'. I liked it and I didn't like it. When we were in front of people and she called me that, it made me feel like a baby, even though I was 14 years old and my real name was Heidi. But I really liked it when we were in private, because I knew she would throw open her arms for me to run into for hugs and kisses. Just like now, she got off Uncle John's lap, and sittin' next to him, she opened her arms wide for me to come and get some lovin'.

Momma's name was Angela, but Uncle John called her Angel. She was so pretty, well, I thought so anyways. She had the prettiest eyes "scarlet, like Elizabeth Taylor's" I heard people say. I never saw pictures or anythin' of her, but she was a beautiful Hollywood actress from the old days, I understand. Momma had the longest, blackest, shiniest hair that I have ever seen, right down to her waist. In the mornin' after her shower, it smelled like pretty flowers, but when she came from work, it smelled of cigarette smoke and liquor, like it did right now. She was a waitress in a bar downtown, "and tha'st the way bars smell," she told me once. My hair was the "the color of corn silk" momma said and lay on my neck and back like a wool blanket and as much as I begged for her to cut it, she refused, tellin' me that between my hair and my green eyes I would hopefully attract a wealthy man and move out of the trailer into a real fine home fit for pretty ladies.

We didn't have no car, so momma would head off around supper time and walk the mile or so into Crockett. That's the name of the town we lived in in Texas. She had to walk home, too, in the middle of the night. Uncle John was always tellin' her that was dangerous, but never did nothin' about it that I could see. He didn't work, and momma didn't mind 'cause he was always 'round to watch me, which saved her payin' for a babysitter.

Uncle John has lived with us for a while now, not like the three other uncles before him. They were pretty nice guys, but two of them fought with momma a lot and I wasn't supposed to see it, but I saw one of them hit her. As each of them left, momma told me one had joined the military, another had to leave the state 'cause he found a job some where's else, and I can't remember where the other went. As long as they didn't mess with her "honey bunny", she didn't mind their stayin' with us.

Uncle John pretty much hung around all day, smokin' cigarettes, watchin' TV, drinkin' beer. He didn't bother me much except maybe to make him some eggs or bring him a beer, things like that. He was so skinny, real tall, had this adam's apple stickin' out of his throat. Mommy told me what it was called, but didn't know why it was named that or what its purpose was. He had skinny, but muscular, arms with all kinds of tattoos. There were protruding dark blue veins running up and down his arms.

I was kinda lonely most of the time. Momma would stay up with me for a little while, usually have some cereal, then she and Uncle John would go into their bedroom at one end of the trailer. Because momma worked, I had a lot of chores: clean up the trailer as best I could, do the laundry which was a chore by itself 'cause we didn't have a washin' machine, take the trash out, pretty much take care of myself and Uncle John. I've been cookin' for a while, nothin' fancy, eggs, hamburger, stuff like that. Besides boxes and boxes of cereal, bread, eggs, chopped meat, that was pretty much all the groceries we had; and of course beer. Once in a while, momma would bring home a chicken and potatoes to roast and freshly baked apple pie for dessert. What a treat that was!

I went to school but wasn't much good at it. The bus would pick me up and drive to Dover Road, right off Main Street in Crokett where the school was. Everythin' seemed so old to me. The school bus was rickety and rusty, faded yellow, bouncin' over ruts in the road, the seats were torn, some sealed with maskin' tape. The bus driver, Mr. Kellerman, was old and fat. His backside hangin' out from both sides of the flatten seat. He did nothin' to make the screamin' kids sit down and behave themselves. Even the schoolhouse was old, three story dull brown building with bars on the windows, small back yard with a few swings and slides for recess and two seesaws, one broken. The yard was dusty on dry days, muddy on wet days. Inside, the corridors and classrooms needed paintin', some walls showin' several coats of previous paint jobs. The desks were low to the ground, pock marked and stained with ink from the old days before ball point pens, a hole on the upper right side where an ink bottle used to sit.

Even the teachers were old. For instance, Mrs. Webber, my math teacher, her hair was kinky with gray tight curls. She was kind of chubby, huge knockers, wore silky looking, busy printed dresses and clunky black shoes with white stockings. She always wore a pair of tiny pearl earrings that were hardly noticeable, buried in her fleshy ear lobes. It wasn't that she was a bad teacher, the other kids seem to know what she was talkin' about, but me, I wondered why I even showed up. I had no plans for college or no higher education at all. As far as I could see, I'd be just like momma. The trailer belonged to grandma who had passed away. Now it was momma and then it would be passed to me.

When I skipped school, I would go down to the stream that ran behind the trailer. Sometimes, when we had heavy rains, the water would come up on land and slowly crawl up towards the trailer like a snake sneaking towards its prey, but so far, we had been lucky. The sun would come out and eventually the water would go down. Mom forbade me to go down to the stream 'cause I might drown, but I couldn't help it. It would get so hot that I had to cool off. When momma would leave for work and Uncle John was inside watchin TV, I would take off all my clothes up to my underwear and go and sit in that stream. When the stream was its normal self, you can sit in it with no trouble and the water would come up to your chest. On days after a big rain, the current was so strong that even a big person like myself, had trouble just sittin'. If you weren't holdin' on to a boulder, it would sweep you away.

I didn't have any friends because I was always busy at home, and to tell the truth, I was ashamed to bring anybody home to the trailer. At one time, when grandma was alive, it was a place I could be proud of. She had planted pretty colorful flowers in front of the trailer and had the local handyman Luther put up a fence around the house, painted it white and put white steppingstones from the house to the gate. For a few dollars and a bottle of booze he would do anything. It was a shame to look at it now. A few brave flowers managed to push their heads through the dirt and pebbles. The white steppingstones were mostly gone, the gate had fallen off and threw away, the fence was hangin' in some places looking like a spotted calf, black and white chipped paint.

I didn't have a grandpa 'cause grandma committed a big, mortal sin when she had a kid without any husband. We didn't much go to church; only Christmas and Easter, but when momma had enough beers in her, she would pull out grandma's bible and read some aloud.

I heard the Catholic kids on the school bus talkin' about me and my family. Turns out my momma had no husband either and I had no papa. That made me a bastard – a kid without a papa – 'cause my momma was a tramp and slept around. They whispered behind their hands, but loud for me to hear. "Here comes Trailer Trash". That was the name they gave me. I would put my head up high and pass them findin' an empty seat in the back of the bus, my cheeks burnin' red like fireplace embers.

Chapter 2

One night, momma didn't come home from work. I had just turned 17. I was sittin' on the couch with Uncle John watchin' wrestlin'. I stopped goin' to school by then and now I could stay up as late as I wanted. I kept watchin' the hands of the clock go round and round and soon it was 2:00 a.m. and no momma. Uncle John didn't seem worried, he being more interested in the wrestlin' matches. I tried a couple of times tellin' him, but he told me not to worry about it and to shut up. That was not like Uncle John. He was always in a good mood and never talked to me that way. He seemed nervous and antsy, like he knew a secret and was dyin' to blurt it out. Somethin' happened yesterday, and I wondered if that had anything to do with momma's being late this mornin'.

Uncle John and momma had a huge fight yesterday. That was strange, too, because they got along real great. I was in my bedroom with earphones on jivin' to some heavy metal rock music. Even though I had it blastin', I could hear raised voices and a couple of times thumpin' as if somebody fell. I opened my door and looked down the corridor. Momma was on the floor and Uncle John was leanin' over her. It took me a minute to realize that he had his hands around her throat and was chokin' the life out of her. I threw down my earphones, ran down the corridor and jumped on Uncle John's back and started beatin' him. He threw me off like I was a fly on a bull's ass. I went flyin', bangin' my head against the woodstove but at least he had stopped hurtin' momma. When momma stood up, her eyes were puffy and one was blackened. I've seen them fight before but this was the worst. He never laid a hand on her ever. There fights were only with words. Uncle John turned to me and shouted, "Ya know what your whorin' mother is doing? She's fuckin Sal for more money in her paycheck." Sal was the owner of the bar where momma worked. "It's all over town, everybody's talkin about it." I wanted to calm him down, so I told him I ain't heard any such thing in town.

Uncle John did a strange thing earlier tonight; he went for a walk. Usually, he sat down with a beer and cigarettes after dinner, and it would take a bomb to get him off the couch. But this time, he suddenly rose from the couch, and announced he was goin' out for some air. I glanced at the clock in amazement. It was almost midnight. I figured maybe he was goin' to meet momma and walk her home. I was so surprised she had even gone to work today with her black eye. But he came back in a half hour without her and momma never came home that night. I asked him if he had seen momma while he was out, but he again told me to shut up, grabbed another beer and fell back into the couch and eventually fell asleep.

I went to my room to escape his loud snorin'. I had no idea what to do. Should I call the police? Should I go out lookin' for her? What if she ran away with Sal? She wouldn't desert me and leave me with Uncle John? Or would she? After the beatin' he gave her last night, I wouldn't blame her for leavin', but she would have taken me with her. Unless Sal didn't like kids.

The sun's rays woke me. My room bathed in brilliance. My first thoughts were confusin': Where I was? Did somethin' happen? Why was I still in my clothes? The events of the previous night grabbed hold of my heart and I ran down to my momma's bedroom at the other end of the trailer. She wasn't there and neither was Uncle John. It was 7:30 in the mornin'. Momma and Uncle John would normally be sleepin'. Somethin' else was strange. Empty drawers were open and so was the closet door. All Uncle John's clothes were gone. He was gone, too. Maybe they eloped, maybe he finally got a job and we all were movin' to another town. When I saw all momma's clothes still there I knew I was thinkin' bullshit. Maybe Uncle John left 'cause he hurt her, maybe she was lyin' in a ditch bleeding. I knew what I had to do.

Chapter 3

It was times like this that I wished we had a car. I hastily walked down the road lookin' in the roadside ditch. A sound I was well familiar with came 'round the bend. It was the school bus. As it passed me, kids were shoutin out the window, "There goes Trailer Trash".

When I finally got to town, I was wet with perspiration. I entered the one-story Crockett Police Station. The air conditioners were blastin' and I could feel my nipples shrivel hard. I stopped at the first desk where a deputy sat. His huge belly hung over his belt, hidin' most of his crotch area, where a split seam was noticeable showin' his white underwear. He looked so uncomfortable behind the small desk. When he looked up to acknowledge me, his face was friendly, his chins round and mushy like baking dough. His eyes were cobalt blue, and his smile revealed crooked teeth but clean and white. He extended his hand in greetin'. "I'm Chucky, what can I do you outta, miss," he chuckled at his own joke.

"My momma didn't come home from work this mornin'," I said, stifling a sob, "and I'm worried sick."

"Where does she work?"

"Crazy Pony."

"Have you been over there to ask Sal Gato what time he closed the joint up last night?"

I shook my head no.

"Is your mom one of the dancers or a waitress?"

"Waitress."

"What's her name?"

"Angela Nolan."

"Oh," Chucky salivated like he was devourin' a steak. "Angela, she's so pretty. She should be a dancer. Probably make a lot more money dancin' than carryin' around those heavy trays, getting her ass pinched. He didn't seem to mind that I was only 17 years and wasn't keen on words like that about my momma."

"What time were you expectin' her?"

"She usually gets in between 1 and 2 a.m."

"Ya know'd anyone who would hurt her?"

I shook my head 'no', but I couldn't erase the sight of Uncle John attackin' her.

"Any husband or boyfriends."

"There's Uncle John who lives with us, but that's all."

"They get along pretty well?"

"Sure," I lied.

"Well, you go home and I'll call Sal later to find out what he knows," he said. "It's too early now, they don't open 'til 6. Leave your phone number and I'll call you later with any information I learn."

He rose from his chair and towered over me in height and width blocking out the light. I noticed the slit in his pants had gained a few smidgens. He walked me to the door on his way to the candy vending machines. His huge hairy hand draped over my shoulder, reminded me of a gorilla's paw.

When I exited the station, I felt so dissatisfied. There had to be more than askin' Sal for information. *Maybe he is responsible for momma disappearance,* I thought, *and if so, he's not gonna offer any information.*

The heat was unbearable, and I dreaded walking home. This time I checked the ditch on the other side of the road. I wondered where Uncle John had gone. I did not want to tell the deputy that he had disappeared because they would probably put me in a foster home. I knew I could take care of myself, having been doing it for years.

When I reached home, the trailer was empty and unbearably hot. I went around turning on useless fans. I was tempted to go swimming in the stream behind the trailer, but it was too low since we did not have any heavy rainfall lately. Instead, I took a cool shower.

Later that day, the deputy called me as promised. He said that quite a few people he interviewed said that most of the night Angela was seen with a well-dressed, city fella, flirtin' with him and givin' him her winnin' smile, bendin' over, puttin' his drink down on the table, temptin' him with her massive breasts. Some of them could swear they saw them drive off in his rich Mercedes. That was impossible. Momma just wouldn't desert me just like that and leave me alone with Uncle John!

And that was the end of the investigation as far as Deputy Chuck was concerned.

Chapter 4

At 17, I lost my virginity. It was a painful experience. It was rape 'for sure. I convinced Sal that I was 18 and he gave me a job waitin' tables at the Crazy Pony. I made enough money to keep myself and the trailer goin' since my wants are simple. One of the patrons had been eyin' me all night long. It gave me a feelin' of power over him, knowin' I had somethin' he desired, and it was the first time a man looked at me that way. I knew I was attractive. Uncle John called me beautiful, which always irritated momma. When I was out by the mailbox and the school bus went by filled with high school kids, I could hear the boys chant: "There Goes Trailer Trash. Who Will Be The First To Give It In Her Ass?" And then raucous laughter. As the bus rounded the curve, I could hear them arguin' who was the stud who would be the first to break my cherry. They sneered as one suggested my cherry was long since broken.

When I left the tavern at closin' time, the stranger followed me out.

"I'm Trevor, who are you?" He was right on my heels.

"That's for me to know and you to find out," I turned, purrin' seductively.

"Oh, you want to play it that way. Where's your car?" he asked.

"Don't have none," I returned.

He reached out and grabbed me, pullin' me closer to him.

"I'm Trevor, what's your name?" he asked again through clenched teeth this time. He was getting mad.

He was tall, about 40, strong, muscular arms, barrel chested, black, wavy hair, black wicked eyes and his face looked like it has been chiseled from stone. I wanted this stranger, wantin' to see what making love felt like.

"I'm Heidi," my voice trembled.

"You walk home so late?" he asked incredulously. "Aren't you afraid? There's a lot of creeps out there."

"I'm not afraid, everybody in town knows me."

"What about guys like me who don't know you, who come from out of town?"

"You not gonna hurt me," I said assuredly. I had this urgent sensation in my crotch area causing me to shiver.

"You cold?" he asked. He took his jacket and offered it to me.

"How can I give it back to you since you don't live around here?"

On the pretense of adjustin' my skirt, I stooped, treatin' him to an eyeful of my breasts.

He licked his lips, ignorin' my question. He draped his jacket around me and gently pulled me toward him. When he kissed me, his tongue roughly pierced my lips, like a serpent searchin' for my tongue. My legs were weak, I hung on to him, his hands gropin' my breasts.

"I'll take you home," he said breathlessly. "Get in the car," he ordered.

I knew I was under his spell, and when I entered his car, I wanted him desperately. The trip home took only a few minutes.

"You live in a trailer?" he said pretentiously, noticing the broken fence and barren landscape. He hesitated before he entered. Once inside, he relaxed. It was tidy and clean.

"Want a beer or coffee?" I asked.

"I don't think so." He grabbed me to himself. "I want you."

"Please be gentle, this is my first time," I whispered.

He burst out laughing.

"You expect me to believe that?" he snickered, pickin' me up and then we started down the corridor, him mutterin' under his breath "That I don't believe." He threw me down on my unmade bed. My body went rigid with terror when he asked me "How ya like it? Up the ass?"

"Don't hurt me, I never done it before," I pleaded hysterically.

He unzipped his fly and let his pants hit the floor. I remember shriekin' when I saw his bulgin' penis. He turned me over on my stomach, then grabbed my hips and situated me up on my knees; my bottom up and facing him. He penetrated me with full force, my screams overlappin' his ecstatic sighs. When he was finish, he turned me over, like a sacrificial lamb, spread my legs and punctured my pussy. I was moanin', screamin', hittin' him with my small fists, tryin' to get him off me, but my movements under him made him more excited and he pumped faster and faster. The torture went on for hours.

Finally, I fell silent, my body went limp. I couldn't take it no more. I wondered when he left, did he notice I had fainted.

Chapter 5

When I finally awoke, he was gone. The lower part of my body throbbed with pain. It hurt so bad just to sit up. My coverings were covered with blood, as were my thighs and private parts. Doubled over, I slowly walked to the bathroom and drew a bath. I made the water as hot as I could stand it, wantin' to wash the smell of him off my body. Lookin' at my body in the full-length mirror, I saw all the bruises and bite marks, especially the one on my left breast that was bleedin'. My face was red and raw in some places, eyes red too, lips bruised. I wondered how long he had been there and what he had done to me after I had fainted because I noticed marks around my wrists that resembled rope burns. I looked down to my ankles. Same thing, rope burns.

Whimperin' and cryin' aloud, I cautiously lowered myself into the hot water, an inch at a time and then I took the washrag and rubbed all traces and smell of Trevor off my body.

After the bath, I desperately wanted a drink. *This is a night of 'firsts'*, I thought. *First screw, first whiskey.* I searched the cabinets until I found a bottle of Uncle John's cheap whiskey and poured myself a full glass with ice cubes. In a panic, I ran to the door and locked it, should

Trevor have any ideas to come back. He had said he would not be here long, so that was a relief. If I ever ran into him again, I wouldn't be so cute and sexy, trying to lead him on. I would just keep my mouth shut and walk on by him.

Sputterin' and coughin', I emptied my glass in one quick swoop and felt the fiery liquid numbin' all my pain. *Horrible tastin' drink,* I thought. I laid down on the couch, coverin' myself with a blanket that always hung on the back of the couch. I started cryin', thinkin' about my momma. Did she desert me? At a time like this I really needed her. Or did Uncle John murder her? With Uncle John gone, it was somethin' I would never know the answer. The whiskey did its job. I fell asleep quickly and painlessly.

The next day, still feelin' the effects of the night before, I called Sal and told him I was sick. He seemed concerned because I never took off. I brushed him off tellin' him it might be a cold comin' on. Since I worked nights, I usually slept 'til 3 p.m. but today I was awake at 9 a.m. *I have a whole day to do what?* I thought about walkin' to town for groceries, but Sal might see me, and I was still spottin' blood.

Instead, I grabbed a bag of chips and a beer, turned on the fan and TV, and dropped onto the couch. The beer tasted a lot better than the whiskey. The happenings of the night before played through my mind like a horror movie. Is that what makin' love is all about? I realized that he showed me no mercy, but I wonder if you loved someone, would it hurt so much even if he was trying to be gentle. She was no angel, having committed the sin of masturbation and had experienced that sensation where you just can't help it. She remembered the intense feeling, her moans and yells escaped in ecstasy; the pleasure was so intense. That's the feeling making love to the man you loved must be like, passionate not painful.

Chapter 6

As I entered the Crazy Pony, my eyes darted to every corner looking for Trevor. I breathed a sigh of relief and went to punch in. *Tonight would be hard,* I thought as I was still sore and wondered if I would be able to carry a full tray.

"Hey beautiful, feelin better?"

It was Sal. In spite of the blastin' air conditioners, he was sweatin'. Beads of sweat had gathered atop his bald head and were runnin' down his fleshy cheeks. His small eyes were lost behind saggin' eyelids and bushy eyebrows. At 50, he had no redeemin' qualities in the looks department and was single, always lookin' and always available. I couldn't imagine him with momma. Uncle John must have heard wrong. Momma would never have takin up with Sal. Momma was loyal, one man at a time and he had to be good lookin'.

"Just some stomach thing," I replied.

"Will you be alright carrying trays and runnin' around the place?"

I nodded yes.

"By the way, I was contacted by the sheriff about your momma. I didn't know nothin' except I did see her leavin with a city guy at the end of the evenin'."

I just couldn't believe that. That was not momma's way of doin' somethin'.

The bar was already crowded this Saturday night. There had been a livestock auction that afternoon in town. Lookin' around, I recognized a lot of the steady customers, but there were many patrons I had never seen before. I grabbed my tray and entered the floor, pulling my low-cut black shirt up a little to try to cover the bite mark on my breast. There were so many customers I had to squeeze passed patrons with my tray held over my head. Whenever there was a livestock auction in town, Sal would hire another waitress to help me out and to keep the drinks movin'. The new waitress was friendly enough. Her name was Marie and she spoke with a Spanish accent. She had black curly hair brushed up in a bun, ringlets hanging to make her look sexy, round black eyes, red kissable lips and a rack that was ready to burst out of its confinement. *She will do well tonight,* I thought.

After a couple of hours of non-stop runnin', I had to sit somewhere and rest; my body was on fire with pain. As Marie ran past carryin' a tray with beers, I signaled her I needed a break.

"You look very pale. Take as much time as you want."

I got a glass of water and went out the back door to sit on the steps. There was already a man sittin' down smokin' a cigarette. I did not recognize him.

"Hey there, pretty lady, you look like you could use a break," he said in a friendly, concerned voice.

My feathers immediately went up. I had to be careful; no more flirtin' with strange men.

"I sure can," I replied, makin' sure I sat a good distance away from him. I hoped he did not want to be chatty because all I could feel was my pain.

"My name is Darryl Hanson. I'm in town for the livestock auction."

I guess because I did not reply and drank my water, he felt he should apologize. "Sorry to intrude on your thoughts, I was just bein' friendly."

"Oh, that's ok, I did not mean to be rude. I just hurt all over." I felt his eyes on the bite mark on my breast and my face turned beat red, so I adjusted my shirt to hide it.

"My name is Heidi Nolan. Ya goin to be here long?"

"Tomorrow is the final auction, then I'll go back home to Waco. I have a huge spread, mostly steers. I come here often for the auctions, don't ever remember seein' you in the Crazy Pony."

"I've only been there a couple of months."

Finishin' my water, I rose. "Well, I have to go, I'm sure Marie is havin' a terrible time by herself."

He stood, his hand extended. My hand was swallowed up in his large, calloused hand.

"Nice to meet you."

When we got to the door, he asked "How about after yer done, we go for coffee. Rosa Café is open all night, maybe a bite to eat, too?" He was tall, blond wavy hair that was a little too long, he had to keep pushin' it aside away from his eyes, his eyes were blue. *So kind*, I thought. I would love to go with him, but I was still fearful after my last experience.

"Thank you, Darryl, but I will be so tired at the end of the night that I would just rather go home."

"How 'bout tomorrow night?"

"No really, I can't, nice to meet you though."

When I came back, Marie glared at me because I was out longer than expected and I came in with a good-lookin' guy.

I grabbed a tray and started takin' orders under the watchful eye of Darryl Hanson who sat at the bar following my every move.

At the end of the evenin', I could hardly move my legs and the thought of the walk home was unbearable. I wondered if Marie would drive me home, but I spotted her talkin' to Darryl Hanson and figured better not disturb her after the glarin' look she had given me earlier. I started walkin' down the road with streaks of pain shootin' up my legs, beads of perspiration dotted my cheeks, and I felt the blood drainin' from my face and was sure I was bleeding down below. A car pulled up on the dark deserted road and I panicked, attemptin' to run, thinking it was Trevor. The bright beams sought me out and the horn was blarin'.

"Hey, Heidi, it's me, Darryl."

I stopped running, thankful for the moment of rest. Even though he had kind eyes, I was still afraid. Who could you trust?

"Hi Darryl, if you're stayin' at the motel, you're goin' the wrong way. It's the opposite way."

"No, I was followin' you. You were practically doubled up your last few hours of work. Look, whatever happened to you is your own business and I won't pry, but you could really use a ride home, and I would be glad to do that for you."

She was convinced that he was referring to the bite on her breast.

"It's not that far. I'm practically there."

"Heidi, get in the car, I'm not going to hurt you," he said with exasperation.

He threw open the car door for me. It was a godsend to sit on the plush seats and smell the newness of the car. To me, it signified sanity, rich businessman who would not hurt me.

"How far do we go?"

"'Bout a quarter of a mile, right around the bend. Here, pull up to this mailbox."

Darryl was confused. He didn't see any houses. He did as I said and pulled up to the mailbox where I painfully crawled out.

"Thank you," I said and went through the downed fence gate. Then he saw the trailer far back on desolate land. It was difficult to see in the dark.

I froze with fear when he asked, "Aren't you goin' to invite me in for a cup of coffee? I realize it's late, but I did you a favor," he chided as they neared the trailer. The outside porch light was on and I again noticed his kind eyes and handsome face. I just knew he would not hurt me.

We went in and Darryl sat at the kitchen table, which was really set up partially in the living room. Looking around he noticed how small the trailer was, probably one of the old ones, 12 x 60, none of the modern conveniences the new ones had.

"I only have instant," I said, turnin' on the kettle.

"That's fine, just wanted a chance to talk to you without all that commotion at the bar. Do you live here alone?"

"Yes."

"No family, no husband, no kids?"

"No."

"You're not a wealth of information," he chuckled, commenting on her short, to-the-point answers.

I brought the two steamin' mugs, set them on the table and took a seat across from him.

"Do you take milk or sugar?"

"No, black is fine."

"No, there's nobody here but me," I finally answered his question.

"Where is your family?"

"My father died when I was really young, and my mother moved to Oklahoma to take care of her ailin' mother," I lied.

"You must be lonely here all by yourself."

"Not really. When I come home from work, I'm exhausted, so I eat my breakfast and go to sleep 'til about 3 when I start getting' ready for work again."

"That's no life for a young girl. You should be out enjoyin' yourself. What days do you have off?"

"Only one, Sundays."

"I was goin' to leave for Waco on Sunday but I can move it to Monday and take you out for a wonderful dinner and then to the Dancin' Boots for some more fun."

I was goin' to refuse his invitation until I saw the excitement in his eyes.

"Sure," I said without hesitation.

"I'll pick you up around 6 tomorrow night." He rose from his chair. I could see that he was surprised by my answer and he went around the table to give me a friendly kiss on my forehead.

And then he was gone, and the trailer seemed so empty without his presence and his voice. I realized how lonely I was; no momma to talk to, to ask advice. No boyfriend like Darryl to cook for, to sleep with, to talk and laugh, his voice echoin' through the trailer. Now there was just silence.

On Sunday mornin', I was sick, retchin' in the toilet sick, the smell of coffee turned my stomach. At first, I fooled myself to thinkin' that it was a virus. When a bite of toast sent me back to the bathroom, sittin' on the floor huggin' the toilet, I admitted to myself what it was. Trevor's baby.

Chapter 7

I wondered if I should call Darryl at the motel and cancel the date. But then I changed my mind, thinkin' I might need him in the future. A devious plan was taking place in my brain. Maybe I would sleep with him and then claimed the baby was his. Life with him would be better than with Trevor or God knows better than being alone in the trailer with an infant. Could I do that to Darryl? It would solve a lot of problems. A father rather than a bastard baby and its mother Trailer Trash. I wanted so badly to be respected and to get rid of that label.

I started to cry. "Momma where are you. I need you now. What should I do? It's hard for me to believe that you left, no looking back, just left me and Uncle John." Then I thought maybe since Uncle John had beat her. I thought this was the new way they would argue because it gets easier the second time.

I could not do that to Darryl. As well as it would solve my problems, it just was not fair to him.

I chose my red dress to wear that also covered the bite on my breast. Whenever I wore this dress, I would get so many compliments. I went to the bathroom to use the mirror to put on some makeup. I was so surprised how haggard I looked. My skin was sallow and brown bags under my eyes added another ten years to my age. I tried to hide them with white cover up and pink rouge to my cheeks. I never had to do anything to my hair as it was naturally wavy.

I heard Darryl's car horn beckonin' me. I grabbed a sweater and went out to greet him. He surprised me with a red rose. I kissed his cheek, surprised by my own carefree action.

Dinner was very nice, conversation was easy. Darryl talkin' about the spread he had in Waco. It consisted of the main house and four cabins for the workers. When he described the main house, it sounded like a mansion to me. He raised thoroughbred Arabian horses, the finest steer in the country and just for fun, goats and lambs. He had ten Mexicans to help with the work, their wives took care of the main house and did the cleanin' and cookin'.

"There's five young 'uns running around always playing' and tumbling' and makin' everyone laugh." The expression in his face changed, lookin' at me with sincerity and earnestness. "I just turned 29. I would love to have some children and a lovin' woman beside me by the time I'm 30."

I felt ashamed by my plan to deceive him.

"Is that somethin' you would be interested in, Heidi? You don't have to answer now, I'll be back in town next month."

"Is this a proposal?" I asked confoundedly. "I just met you."

"It is if you want it to be. Heidi, I know you care for me, I see it in your eyes. We are meant to be together."

"I'm only 18," I protested.

"But you think like a woman and I'm sure you feel like a woman in my arms."

After dinner, we went to the Dancin' Boots where we danced, drank and laughed and had a wonderful time. The last dance was a slow one. He took me in his arms and held my body so close to his that I felt his erection. At the end of the dance, he kissed my lips. I knew then I could never leave this man.

When we got to the trailer, Darryl came in. He grabbed me close to him and hungrily kissed my lips. Picking me up, we went down the hallway to my room where he gently laid me down on the bed. He undid my blouse and gently kissed my breasts, my stomach. I felt my body respond, hungerin' sighs and moans escaped my lips. He slipped my dress off and unzipped his pants. I could not help it. I was tearing at his shirt tryin' to get it off so we would be skin to skin. Then the most wonderful sensation I have ever felt. He was kissing my pussy. I writhed and twisted, guttural sounds escaped involuntary from my throat as I came.

Suddenly, I bolted up, "Darryl, please go, just go please."

"What's the matter?" he asked, confused.

"We shouldn't have done this."

"Why not, I love you. You seemed to have a great time with me tonight."

"We could see each other next month when you come again." I grabbed my robe off a nearby chair and walked him out to his car.

"Can I kiss you goodnight at least?"

His kisses were soft and gentle. Darryl put his hand into his breast pocket and pulled out a business card. "This is for you, if you ever want to call me. All my information is on it. I'd love to hear from you."

He placed a kiss onto my forehead, got into the car and he drove away. My final thought was, *so that's what gentle love feels like.*

Chapter 8

I never called Darryl, but I have to admit he was always on my mind. I decided not to straddle him with a bastard kid. He was just such a good man and didn't deserve to have this cruel joke played on him. The pregnancy wasn't showing yet and it was my fourth month. The morning sickness was over, and I was still able to keep up at work. Darryl would come in once a month, and last month when I told him it was my birthday, he brought a beautiful bouquet and a diamond ring as gifts. I looked at the ring quizzingly and he assured me it wasn't an engagement ring, just a friendship ring. I couldn't forget his proposal and didn't think it was just a friendship ring.

When Darryl came to town, he would stay at the trailer for the one night. I felt like I was married, sleepin' together, me makin' breakfast, our conversations. It wasn't lonely and empty anymore.

By the sixth month, the pregnancy became obvious. I didn't want Darryl to know and told him I had to work seven days the next couple of months. He said he was busy with foaling this time of year and since I was workin', would skip the next few months. People in town noticed it. Sal wanted to know who the father was, but I never told him. He let me go in the eight month and hired Marie full-time.

I was so depressed and uncomfortable. I didn't want this baby, conceived in hate. Will I become my mother, livin' with different men, work at the bar if Sal would hire me back, have an uncle watch the kid while I was workin? I wondered how my momma did it, who was my father? She seemed happy in the life she had chosen for herself, but now I was ashamed of her. It was her fault I was called Trailer Trash and now I was livin' up to my reputation and I hated her for that. Today I went into town to apply for welfare and food stamps.

The baby was movin' around in my womb causing severe contractions. I had no plans for a hospital birth. How bad could it be. There were women all over the world who had natural childbirth?

Even though I was ashamed of my mother, I wished she could be here with me, holdin' my hand, coachin' me through the birth. I wondered if she would think of herself as grandma. I had so many questions to ask her.

I wish it could be different and it was Darryl's baby. I could live in the big house with Darryl and our baby, a perfect family.

What a wonderful life it would be, but I missed my chance. I'm damned to spend my days in this trailer trap. I really screwed up my life. But it wasn't my fault; he raped me. But I encouraged it by being flirty when I told him 'That's for me to know and you to find out'. I should have gone to the sheriff office, then people would know I was raped, not a tramp, just a young girl who ran into some bad luck. The towns' people would feel sorry for us and help her out in various ways and stop calling her Trailer Trash.

On a Saturday night, my water broke all over the couch. I read some books about birthing babies, but I knew I really weren't ready. I grabbed a scissor from the kitchen drawer and a bowl of hot water and rag to bathe the baby and stumbled down the hallway to my room. The pain was coming every two minutes.

I spread some old blankets and a pillow on the floor since I didn't want to mess up my bed linens. Layin' down I waited. The pains were unbearable. Nature took over and I began to pant and push. I could feel the baby's head in between my legs. I gave one mighty scream and push and the baby was out. For one instant I thought it might be a still birth because I heard no whimpering, but now the baby was movin' and cryin'. It took whatever strength I had to sit up, take the scissor and cut the umbilical cord and wipe all the afterbirth off the baby. It was a girl. I just wanted to sleep but she wouldn't stop cryin'. I wrapped her in a blanket and put her to my breast and she started to suckle. That's the way we both fell asleep.

Chapter 9

Months had passed. Darryl, sensin' my disinterest, stopped comin' to town and took his business elsewhere. I was just pretendin' I wasn't interested. I didn't want him comin' and seein' the way I lived. Every room in the trailer were jammed packed with dirt, clothin', diapers, empty baby bottles and beer bottles. I couldn't afford those diapers you see on TV, so I had to use cloth diapers. Since I didn't have a washin' machine, I had to wash them by hand, but I wasn't so good about doin' the laundry as often as I should. How did momma do it? Then I figured she always had a man in the house to help. But that wasn't true. All the uncles that passed through had nothin to do with me. Even Uncle John was a poor excuse for a father. He wasn't a father and didn't want to be one.

Even my personal hygiene suffered. I would take a shower now and again when I couldn't stand my own stink. My hair was disheveled and many a time I thought about cuttin' it all off. The baby, I named Angela after my mother. She kept me up most nights. I didn't know if it was from diaper rash, hunger or maybe she was ailin'. I didn't take to motherhood very well; bein' depressed all the time. Angela was pretty smart. She was already crawlin' and sort of walkin' in her eighth month.

Goin' to town was such a pain. I only went once a month when my welfare check and my food stamps came. At least I had the carriage to put the groceries in when comin' from the supermarket.

I was so ashamed on the checkout line. Not only because I had to give the clerk the stamps, but the people on line after me were cluckin' and bitchin' because I was takin' so long. I heard whispered comments about 'how their hard-earned money was going to Trailer Trash who needed food stamps to buy food but had her own money to buy her beer'.

I did have a few boyfriends, mostly those I met at the supermarket, since I went nowhere else and the guys in town who knew they could have a beer and a lay at the trailer on Miller Road. Some of the guys in the supermarket were high school age but I didn't care. I could get arrested for giving minors alcohol and having sex with minors. But nobody said anythin' probably because they were getting' laid and drinkin' beer for nothin'. After a young 'un left, I would feel terrible, like a real tramp but I had needs, not just fer sex but I needed some conversation bein' around my kid all the time.

Darryl would call me occasionally, but we really had nothin' to say to each other anymore. I lied and told him I was still working at the Crazy Pony and everythin' was great. I told him about this wonderful man named Frank who I met there and we were now livin' together and talkin' about marriage. I thought I heard a gasp when I mentioned that to him.

One early afternoon, I was slightly tipsy after a few beers, sitting on the couch thinkin'. Angela was walkin' her Frankenstein type walk up and down the living room, sucking on a piece of bread. I was tryin' to come up with a plan to get out of this life I hated and join Darryl in the main house on his homestead. There was a powerful thunderstorm outside as I sat there plannin'. Torrents of raindrops pounded the metal trailer like machine gun fire. I rose from the couch to get another beer. Now I'm not a bad woman, never have been, never was, but something took hold of me like the devil enterin' my mind and body.

Watching Angela clumsily walkin' up and down, that annoyin' babbling' that she did, a plan came together. I finally knew what I was goin' to do. The first part of the plan would be to call Darryl. I put Angela in the bedroom with her teddy bear and another slice of bread to keep her quiet so Darryl would not hear her. The second part of my plan involved Angela; she would have to go in a way that no one would suspect foul play. I knew the stream had overflowed its banks in this violent storm. I couldn't imagine myself holdin' her head down into the water. It has to look like an accident.

Chapter 10

I found the business card Darryl had left with me. My stomach was quiverin'. He picked the phone up on the second ring.

"Hello."

It was wonderful to hear is voice again. It had been so long since we had spoken.

"Darryl, it's me, Heidi,"

He seemed alarmed.

"Heidi, is anythin' wrong? Are you ok?"

"I'm fine, I really am. How are you?"

"I'm good, you sound wonderful, Heidi."

"Darryl, I realize I don't love Frank. It's you I love and if you still want me, I'll come to you as soon as I can. I think about you day and night. I remember how nice it was when you stayed here overnight, how we made love, and I would lay in your arms feelin' so protected and loved."

I held my breath waiting for his answer.

"Of course, I want you, Heidi. I was so upset when you said you were marryin' some guy named Frank."

On the pretense that Frank was a real person, I told Darryl that it was all a mistake, I didn't really love him. It's you I wanted to spend the rest of my life with.

I saw Angela crawling out of the bedroom, so I had to hang up fast before she started babbling again.

"Darryl, I checked the train schedule. There's a train that leaves Odessa early Sunday morning that stops at Waco," I said. "It comes in at 5:10 p.m. When I get there, I'll call you to come and get me. I can probably be there next week. There's nothing to do here. I could just desert the trailer. I'm so behind on property taxes, the town will probably destroy it and sell the property."

And that's the way we left it.

I went into the bathroom and filled up the tub with soapy water. Taking a pile of soiled diapers, I put them in the tub and started to scrub them. Angela stayed close at hand watching what I was doing. When the diapers were finally clean, I put them in a laundry basket. No wonder I didn't do this job too often, it was disgusting. The weather forecast was on the TV. Tomorrow was going to be bright and sunny and I knew the stream would have overflowed its banks from the thunderstorm that had just rumbled by. Everything was perfect.

Chapter 11

The next day was just like the weatherman had predicted, bright and sunny. The stream had overflowed its bank during the violent thunderstorm the night before and was creeping toward the trailer. I took the laundry basket outside along with a bag of clothespins, Angela and her colored beach ball.

Two young boys passed the trailer with their fishing poles. I panicked; they saw me out in the yard with Angela. Then I relaxed. That's the best thing that could have happened. Two kids going fishin' saw me and Angels out in the yard and I was hangin' laundry. They would verify my statement; accidental death.

As I hung the diapers, I kept my eye on her as she played with her ball rollin' it towards the water. She stood up a couple of times, but fell down on her rear, sitting in muddy water. The stream grabbed her ball and was taking it downstream. She screamed and stood again and walked into the water up to her knees when she fell. She went under a few times, gaspin' and chokin', and finally the torrents of water took her downstream along with her ball. I made not a move to save her.

As a mother, you would think I had changed my mind watchin' my own flesh and blood strugglin' in surgin' water, but I felt nothin'. I was surprised how quickly it went. The gushing' stream grabbed her and took her just like that. I waited a few minutes before I went into the house to call Sheriff Johnson. One thing everybody always said about the Sheriff was that he was always fair. I grabbed a beer and sat at the kitchen table sippin' and thinkin' about what I had just done. Should I go down the embankment to make sure she had drowned before I called the Sheriff? That's probably the better thing to do. I put my beer back into the refrigerator, put my boots on and started down the embankment to where I thought she had landed. I didn't see her at first but then I saw her tangled in the underbrush. "Angela, I shouted, Angela, it's mommy." She actually looked like a life-sized doll. Her blue eyes were open and her skin was like porcelain, her cheeks pink. I took a long stick and poked her; there was no reaction. I never saw the two boys fishin' across the stream on the other side watchin' me.

When I got back to the trailer, I took off my boots and got my beer again. I was tryin' to calm myself before I called Sheriff Johnson. Takin' a deep breath, I gave an academy award performance on the phone, screamin', weepin', shoutin' like a good mother would.

When all the cars and people came, I was down by the stream. I ran towards the Sheriff and threw myself into his arms, weepin' hysterically.

"I was hanging wash; she was playin' with her ball behind me." I took some breaths before I continued. "There wasn't a sound, no cryin', no callin' mommy, nothin'. It just swallowed her up. When I turned, she was gone."

The Sheriff patted me on my hand.

"I thought she was still here, so I searched around callin' her name thinkin' she went into the trailer." The tears rolled down my cheeks non-stop. "I went into the trailer, but she wasn't there. I went to the edge of the stream callin her name and then I saw her beach ball further down in the stream. I just took my eyes off Angela for a minute and the stream swallowed her up and carried her away."

Men were already searchin' for her downstream. About fifteen minutes later, there was a yell from one of the responders that they had found the body entangled in some branches along the shoreline. I fell to the ground in a faint.

The followin' days were hectic. Sal took up a collection to help with funeral expenses and a little extra for me. People I didn't even know attended the funeral way over twenty-five at least. There was a reception at the firehouse in town. After greetin' and talkin' to so many mourners, I was exhausted.

Deputy Chucky drove me home in the patrol car and handed me a check for $2,000. "The townspeople wanted you to have a little somethin' to get you by."

I was amazed by the generosity.

The first thing I did when I got home was have a beer. I had already figured out what I would use the money for; a brand-new wardrobe, a beauty shop appointment and the fare to Waco. I called Darryl on Friday to let him know my train was coming into Waco at 5:15 on Sunday. We both were so excited.

On Saturday, I called a cab from a neighboring town and walked out of that trailer for the last time. I had my hair done and bought my wardrobe in another town so as not to be seen in Crockett.

When I got to Waco, Darryl was there waitin' for me. We embraced and kissed with such joy. He helped me into his SUV and we began our trip to his homestead.

The landscape was beautiful. We passed fields, green hills, lakes, and majestic homes. After about three miles, we pulled off the highway and onto a dirt road. A white, picket fence ran along the road on both sides and the road was lined with weeping willow trees. When we exited the grotto of long, green tresses from the weeping willows into the bright sunshine, there it was, the beautiful main house. It was two stories, white, surrounded by a wrap-around porch, the windows were floor to ceiling and a bricked curved driveway was in front of the house. Lattice work adorned the eaves. The house was surrounded by rose bushes of every color their perfume permeated the still air. There were miles of white fencing surrounding beautiful pastures that resemble plush green carpet. Ten magnificent Arabian horses were grazing. The property was dotted with small houses where the ranch hands lived. Further up behind the pastures were grasslands with his prize steers. Lambs and goats ran freely on the lawn.

He picked me up and carried me to the red door and over the threshold like a bride. On the right was the living room, furnished with two blue sofas, a few high back chairs, mahogany coffee table, well-worn pink and blue carpet, antique lamps and a piano. Straight ahead was the wooden staircase to the upstairs bedrooms. The kitchen was huge and had all the latest cooking equipment and was very modern. The dining room was very formal, long dining room table that could fit twelve comfortably, a crystal chandelier over the table, China closet with colored glass pieces. This was the only room where the walls were painted, baby blue paint, with wainscoting, the bottom was navy blue.

Darryl pulled me toward him and gave me a passionate kiss.

"Let's go upstairs. I want you so badly."

He led me to the master suite, California king bed, black, spindle head and foot boards, yellow quilting.

We just entered the room, and we were already undressing, pulling at each other's clothes. When we were naked, he laid on the bed and gently pulled me on top of him. I straddled his swollen penis and began to rock back and forth. Darryl had my breasts in his hand gently pinching my hardened nipples. I kissed him hungrily, searchin' for his tongue. He started to move up and down, moanin' in ecstasy. I matched his movements and suddenly we both cried out in guttural voices and when it was over, I collapsed into his arms. We both fell asleep.

Chapter 12

The first week was heavenly. After breakfast we would tour the ranch. The horses were majestic, tall, sleek, galloping around their pastures. He introduced me to the ranch hands and their wives and children. It was such a happy place; everybody cheerful and friendly. They welcomed me into the family. When they were inspectin' the steer enclosure, Darryl mentioned that this weekend he wanted to go to the steer auction in Crockett.

A feeling of dread passed over me. How could I keep my secret? People would flock around me offering me their condolences for the death of my daughter. Should I make up a story to tell Darryl, I was raising Angela's daughter who drowned in the stream. That wouldn't work, everybody knew it was my child observing my swollen belly as I walked through town.

Every night we would eat a gourmet dinner prepared by Lolita, wife of Pedro, the ranch manager accompanied by cabernet wine from the wine cellar downstairs. Sometimes she would bring her five-year-old grandson Jose with her. Darryl's face would light up when he saw him. He had a supply of toy trains for Jose to play with, many times getting on the floor and together they would play with the trains.

Seein' Darryl & Jose play was heartwarming. What would he think if he knew what I had done? After dinner, they would go out and sit on the rockers on the wrap around porch planning their future. They would end the night in each other's arms, making sweet, gentle love.

Darryl's plan was we leave early Friday, stay at the Crockett motel, go to the auction on Saturday and then go where we went on our first date, Crazy Pony and then dancin' at the Dancin' Boots. I didn't know what to do, pretend I'm sick Friday & Saturday and stay at the motel? I had forgotten that he was a regular at the auctions in Crockett, how could I have forgotten that detail?

Chapter 13

We were on the road at 6:00 a.m. He was in such a good mood. I asked my fear by forcing myself to concentrate on what he was saying, smilin' or laughin' at the appropriate place.

I never realized how much I hated that town until we pulled up to the motel. Mrs. Hasby wasn't at her usual place behind the counter. A young girl gave us our room and our key. We unpacked and soon it was dinnertime.

"Hungry? I know I'm starving because we rode right through lunch."

"Hmm."

"What's the name of that fancy restaurant on James Street?"

"Pleasant Valley."

"Why don't we call them and see if they can fit two people in for dinner?" The maître de said she could take us in a half-hour. "Since we have some time to kill, want to go to Crazy Pony and visit Sal?"

"No!" My response sounded sharper than how I intended it to sound.

"Well, what do you want to do for a half hour? Want to go see the old trailer. Did you get everything you wanted out of it?"

"Darryl, I don't have any happy memories from this place. If you don't mind, I don't want to come here when you go to auctions,"

I saw the disappointment in his face.

"Are you sure you want to go to dinner at Pleasant Valley, or do you want to skip that too?" he said sarcastically.

I tried to sound agreeable, "Of course. I'm starving, too."

Dinner was uneventful. Nobody stared or came over to offer condolences. We had a very nice time and the earlier friction was forgotten.

We made love that night, but it didn't feel right in this motel; this bed that was shared by hundreds of people.

We arose early because Darryl wanted to go and examine the steer to decide which ones he would bid on.

As we were picking our way cautiously around pens, a familiar voice called out to me, "Heidi," I pretending I didn't hear him.

"Heidi," more forceful this time.

"Hi, Sal," Darryl and I said in unison.

"They got some good animals today at the auction. It's gonna be very competitive. How you feelin' Heidi?"

"Fine."

"You must stop in the Sheriff office today. He wanted to talk to you again, but he didn't know where you went. You disappeared so quickly."

"What this about?" Darryl asked.

My heart was poundin' in my chest.

"The baby."

"What baby?" Darryl was perplexed.

"Heidi's. Didn't she tell you 'bout it?"

They were interrupted by the loudspeaker calling all bidders to the arena.

"I don't want to miss this auction. We'll talk later." Darryl was somber.

He couldn't concentrate on what he was doing and didn't bid on any of the animals.

They were on their way to the motel when Darryl said, "I want to stop into Crazy Pony and talk to Sal unless you have something you want to tell me."

"Let's go to the bar in the motel Darryl and I'll tell you everything."

I had two mixed drinks to give me the courage to go on. I told him about the rape, the pregnancy, and the death of the baby. He was so sympathetic to me, takin' me into his arms, "Heidi, how awful, why did you not tell me before?"

I started sobbin'. "I couldn't, I don't like thinkin' about it. It was too painful."

"Why does the Sheriff want to see you?"

"Probably just a loose end."

"We can go over to the station and see if he's still there?"

"I'm too tired and emotionally drained. Why don't I just call him when we get home?"

Chapter 14

We got up early Sunday morning. Darryl was still in the shower and I was blow dryin' my hair when there was a sharp knock on the door, causin' me to jump in shock. Darryl came out of the bathroom. "Who could that be at 9 a.m. on a Sunday mornin'?" He put a bathrobe on and answered the door. There was Deputy Chuck and Sheriff Johnson.

"Sorry to call on you so early but we have questions for you, Heidi, concerning the death of your baby," Sheriff Johnson said. "Mind if we sit?" Deputy Chuck didn't have his jovial smile today. Sheriff Johnson pulled out the chair from the desk. Deputy Chuck chose the easy chair, leaving me and Darryl to sit on the bed together.

"Tell me again what happened that morning, Heidi. The morning of the *accident*."

I thought, *I don't like the way he said accident*. "It's very simple, I was hangin' diapers on the line, Angela was behind me, I turned to check on her and she was gone. I thought she was in the house…"

"Just a moment, how old is she?"

"Eight months."

"You thought your 8-month-old daughter walked to the house, opened the door and went in?"

"Well, I wasn't thinking right because I was so frightened." I started to cry; my nerves getting the best of me. Darryl took my hand for encouragement.

"Then what did you do?"

"I ran down to the stream, I saw the beach ball down the stream a ways, I ran down there and I saw Angela in the underbrush. I poked her to see if she was alive. Then I ran back to the house to call you."

"What would you say if I told you we have witnesses who saw the whole incident and saw Angela enter the stream and when she fell, you did nothing?"

Darryl dropped my hand. I could feel his eyes burnin' through me. I couldn't believe he deserted me that quickly.

"Are they reliable witnesses?" Darryl asked,

"Two teenagers fishing from the opposite side of the stream; one of them is the preacher's son."

He rose from the bed, went towards the door and turned to look at me one last time. His eyes showed disbelieve, pain, hatred. He didn't say anything; he just walked out of my life.

Chapter 15

The trial was a sensation. Nothin' like this ever happened and finally the residents of Crockett had something to talk about. My court appointed defense lawyer did the best he could, but how do you go against two witnesses, one a preacher's son. I got life without the possibility of parole. I never thought I would say this, but I wished I was back in the trailer.

The newspapers gave reference to my nickname Trailer Trash and some of the prisoners called me that. I didn't mind it anymore, better than bein' called a murderer. I can't believe how far down I came. I had a taste of the good life for a week with Darryl in that beautiful house. But I guess when you are born Trailer Trash, you stay that way forever. Nothin' you can do about it.